Black Lagoon
Favorites

The Teacher from the Black Lagoon
The Principal from the Black Lagoon
The Cafeteria Lady from the Black Lagoon
The School Bus Driver from the Black Lagoon

by Mike Thaler · pictures by Jared Lee

SCHOLASTIC INC.   Cartwheel B·O·O·K·S®

New York Toronto London Auckland Sydney
Mexico City New Delhi Hong Kong Buenos Aires

The Teacher from the Black Lagoon, ISBN 0-590-41962-5,
Text copyright © 1989 by Mike Thaler. Illustrations copyright © 1989 by Jared D. Lee Studio, Inc.

The Principal from the Black Lagoon, ISBN 0-590-45782-9,
Text copyright © 1993 by Mike Thaler. Illustrations copyright © 1993 by Jared D. Lee Studio, Inc.

The Cafeteria Lady from the Black Lagoon, ISBN 0-590-50493-2,
Text copyright © 1998 by Mike Thaler. Illustrations copyright © 1998 by Jared D. Lee Studio, Inc.

The School Bus Driver from the Black Lagoon, ISBN 0-439-06750-2,
Text copyright © 1999 by Mike Thaler. Illustrations copyright © 1999 by Jared D. Lee Studio, Inc.

12 11 10 9 8 7 6 5 4 3 2 1   5 6 7 8 9 10/0
Printed in the U.S.A.   24
This edition created exclusively for Barnes & Noble, Inc.
2005 Barnes & Noble Books
ISBN 0-7607-9539-8
First compilation printing, May 2005

The Teacher
from the
Black Lagoon

It's the first day of school.
I wonder who my teacher is.

I hear Mr. Smith has dandruff and warts,

and Mrs. Jones has a whip and a wig.

But Mrs. Green is supposed to be a *real* monster.
Oh my, I have *her*!
Mrs. Green…room 109.
What a bummer!

I sit at a desk.
I fold my hands.
I close my eyes.
I'm too young to die.

Suddenly a shadow covers the door.
It opens....

In slithers Mrs. Green.
She's *really* green!

She has a tail.
She scratches her name on the blackboard—with her claws!

Freddy Jones throws a spitball.

She curls her lip and breathes fire at him.
Freddy's gone.

There is just a little pile of ashes on his desk.

"Talk about bad breath," giggles Eric Porter.

She slithers over, unscrews his head,
and puts it on the globe stand.

I bet she gives homework the first day of school.

"Your homework for today," grins Mrs. Green,
smoke rising from her nostrils,
"is pages 1 to 200 in your math book—
all the fraction problems."

"We've never had fractions," shouts Derek Bloom.
"Come up here," she beckons with her claw.

Derek stands by her desk.
"This is a whole boy," she smirks.

She takes a big bite.
"This is half a boy. Now you've had fractions."

Doris Foodle cracks her gum.

Mrs. Green swallows her in one gulp!
"No chewing in class," she smiles.

Mr. Bender, the principal, sticks his head in.
"Keep up the good work,"
he nods and closes the door.
I wish I could get sent to the principal's office.

"Let's call the roll," cackles Mrs. Green.
"Freddy Jones is absent.
Derek Bloom is half here.
Eric Porter is here and there.
Doris Foodle is digesting."

"What about spelling?" shouts Randy Potts.
"Spelling can be *fun*!" beams Mrs. Green,
wiggling her fingers at him.

"Abracadabra Kazam!"
"That's tough to spell," says Randy.
Suddenly there's a flash of light, a puff of smoke,
and Randy's a frog.

Penny Weber raises her hand.
"Can I go to the nurse?" she whines.
"What's wrong?" asks Mrs. Green.
"I have a huge headache," says Penny.

Mrs. Green wriggles her fingers. There's another flash of light, and Penny's head is the size of a pin.

"Better?" asks Mrs. Green.

"Now it's naptime. Everyone who still has one, put your head on your desk."

I hope I make it to recess.
"Sweet dreams," she cackles as I close my eyes.

Suddenly the bell rings.
I wake up.
There's a pretty woman writing her name
on the blackboard.

She has real skin and no tail.
"I'm Mrs. Green, your teacher," she smiles.

I jump out of my chair, run up, and hug her.
"Well, thank you," she says, "I'm glad to be here."

Not as glad as I am!

The ~~Teacher~~ Principal
from the
Black Lagoon

It's the third day of school.
I've been sent to the principal's office. What a bummer!

I hear the principal, Mrs. Green, is a real monster.

Kids go to her office and never come back.

The waiting room is supposed to be filled with bones and skeletons.

Doris Foodle was sent there for chewing gum.

They say her skeleton still has a bubble in its mouth.

I walk in.
I take a seat.
The rug is red.
That's so the blood won't show.

I hear she uses tall kids as coat racks.

The short kids she feeds to her pet alligator.

The fat ones she uses as paperweights.

The thin ones she uses as bookmarks.

I'm too young to be a bookmark!

Then there's her twelve-foot paddle.
It's supposed to have poisoned spikes on it.

If you're lucky you get put in "the cages."
She has them under her desk.

If you're *really* lucky you get sent home in chains.

But most kids she keeps for her *experiments*.

Derek Bloom was sent here yesterday.
They say he wound up with the head of a dog.

They say Freddy Jones has the feet of a chicken,

and Eric Porter, the hands of a hamster.

I'm too good-looking to have the ears of a rabbit!

All I did was snatch Mrs. Jones's wig.

It's very quiet today.
Usually, they say, there's a lot of screaming.
Maybe she's in a good mood.

Even if I survive, this will affect my whole life.

In the future I'll be running for president.
I'll be ahead in the polls.

And then it will come out!

I can see the headlines...

Oh-oh, there's a shadow at the glass.
Now I'm in the *jaws of fate*.

The door slowly opens.

There's a pretty woman standing there.
She's a master of disguise.

"Come in, Hubie."

I go in.
She closes the door behind me.

I look around.
There's only the coat rack.
It doesn't look like anyone I know.

I look around for the alligator.
There's only a turtle.
It looks a little like Randy Potts.

"Now," says Mrs. Green. "Are we having a little trouble in class?"
"Well," says I, "I was sweeping up the room and by accident
 Mrs. Jones's wig got caught on the broom handle."

"Well, we'll have to apologize, won't we?"

"Yes, we will."

"And the next time, *we'll* have to be more careful."

"Yes, we will! Yes, we will!"

"Now run along."

"Is that *all*???"

"Close the door."

Boy, was I lucky.
Those flowers on her desk were probably poisonous.
Just one whiff and you would turn purple and die.
Fortunately I held my breath.

I went into her cave and I have returned without the ears of a rabbit.

I'll have to sweep *her* office sometime and see if *she* wears a wig!

The Cafeteria Lady
from the
Black Lagoon

We got a new cafeteria lady today.
Her name is Wanda Belch.

Eric says that instead of a car, she drives
a garbage truck to school.

Freddy heard that she learned to cook on a pirate ship, so don't go near the kitchen.

Derek says that at Wanda's old school, kids found sneakers and baseball caps in her tuna surprise.

And when class pets disappeared...

The kids made sure to check the specials the next day.

All the kids say that Wanda uses natural ingredients
in her dishes: organic rats in her *ratatouille*...

sweaty socks in her *moussaka*...

gooey ghouls in her *goulash* . . .

real sand and witches in her sandwiches.

We've heard Wanda's into recycling.
The water she washes the dishes in will be ...

tomorrow's soup of the day.

I heard she doesn't throw *anything* away!

I wonder what Wanda's cooking up right now?
Today's menu will probably be:

ROADKILL RAVIOLI

SPAGHETTI WITH BOWLING BALLS

SOUFFLÉ OF SCIENCE EXPERIMENTS
and TOXIC WASTE TACOS

For dessert we might have ton cake,
which is pound cake . . .

only heavier.

Even if you can't eat the food, they say
it's always good for something.
The meatballs are aerodynamic...

the mashed potatoes are good for sculpting...

the pudding will stick to anything . . .

and the spinach is great for vinyl repairs.

I hope the spaghetti will make good shoelaces.

Uh-oh, it's time for lunch!
I'm too young to die.
Can't we have a math test instead?
Isn't it time for vaccinations?

We're being lined up and marched down to the *cafetorium*.

I'll bet Wanda's stirring up poisonous pots
full of molten messes of steamy slime.

We're through the door.
We get our trays.
They don't even offer us blindfolds.

Hey! Wanda doesn't look so bad.
And look! She made hamburgers and french fries.

They smell good if you take your hand off your nose.
I'm going to get two!

Gobble, gobble, munch, munch.
Look out, stomach, here comes lunch!
Hey, these taste great!
Maybe I'll get three more.

There are even homemade chocolate-chip
cookies for dessert!
Lunchtime is going to be my favorite class.

Maybe Wanda will let us stay for dinner?

The School Bus Driver
from the
Black Lagoon

We're getting a new bus driver this morning.
His name is T. Rex Fenderbender.
I wonder if the "T" stands for "Tyrannosaurus."

Eric heard that he's really a *cruel* bus driver and drives the *Magic Ghoul Bus.*

And Derek heard he lets his guide dog do most of the driving.

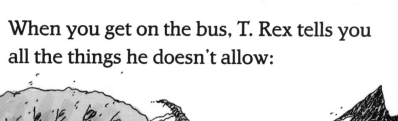

When you get on the bus, T. Rex tells you
all the things he doesn't allow:

Then he tells you that your seat cushion can be used as a flotation unit in the unlikely event of a water landing.

The kids say that sometimes T. Rex drives like he's in the Indy 500...

or the demolition derby...

when he's not practicing for
the Monster Truck Show.

Driving to school can be a *real* drag.
And when he puts on his helmet and shouts,
"Let's see what this baby can do!" you'll
wish you hadn't eaten breakfast.

I heard he collects stop signs and parking meters.

He thinks the school bus is an off-road vehicle,
and that you're less likely to hit another car
if you're on the sidewalk.

He not only *stops* at all railroad tracks—
he *drives* on them!
Getting there is *not* half the fun!

Freddie says that if there's a flat,
we have to change the tire.

If the engine breaks down, *we* have to fix it.

And he makes *us* pay for the gas out of our lunch money.

Randy says sometimes he gets lost — and won't ask for directions until you're in the boondocks.

Eventually, they say, you make it to school.

But he doesn't stop.
You have to jump out...while he's moving!

Uh-oh. There's the bus!
It's stopping for me.
The door's opening.

Hey, he doesn't look so bad.
I guess he left his dog at home today.
He smiles and lets me sit up front.
Then he closes the door, turns off the flasher,
pulls in the stop sign, and slowly drives away.

Boy, I wish he'd go faster—
I've never been in the Indy 500!